To Melinda and John F., with love —L. L.

For Mick and Ginny, and all the little monsters next door —D. P.

Text © 2003 by Laura Leuck.
Illustrations © 2003 by David Parkins.

Book design by Kristen M. Nobles.
Typeset in Amigo.
The illustrations in this book were rendered in acrylic and alkyd paints on acrylic painting paper.
Manufactured in Hong Kong.

Library of Congress Cataloging-in-Publication Data
Leuck, Laura.
Jeepers creepers : a monstrous ABC / by Laura Leuck ; illustrated by David Parkins.
p. cm.
Summary: Twenty-six monsters go to school and learn their letters as each one's name starts with another letter of the alphabet.
ISBN 0-8118-3509-X
[1. Monsters-Fiction. 2. Alphabet. 3. Stories in rhyme.] I. Parkins, David, ill. II. Title.
PZ8.3.L54943 Je 2003
[E]—dc21
2002013240

Distributed in Canada by Raincoast Books
9050 Shaughnessy Street, Vancouver, British Columbia V6P 6E5

10 9 8 7 6 5 4 3 2 1

Chronicle Books LLC
85 Second Street, San Francisco, California, 94105

www.chroniclekids.com

Jeepers Creepers

A Monstrous ABC

by Laura Leuck * illustrated by David Parkins

chronicle books · san francisco

A Ann has alligator skin.

B

Bud grows toadstools on his chin.

Cody's belly button glows.

D

Drew blows beetles from his nose.

Ed's hair smells like sauerkraut.

Freddy's two front fangs fell out.

Gert wears crawdads in her ears.

Hal's head often disappears.

Ida's back has slippery scales.

I

Jane has corkscrew fingernails.

K Kendra's tail is spiked and strong.

Lucy's tongue is ten feet long.

M

Marilyn has spider legs.

Nelson's neck has bolts and pegs.

Oliver has vulture wings.

Peggy has a thumb that stings.

Sid has fifteen purple toes.

Tommy's red eyes never close.

U

Ursula has lizard lips.

Vicky's horns have neon tips.

Winifred breathes flames of fire.

Xavier wears tape attire.

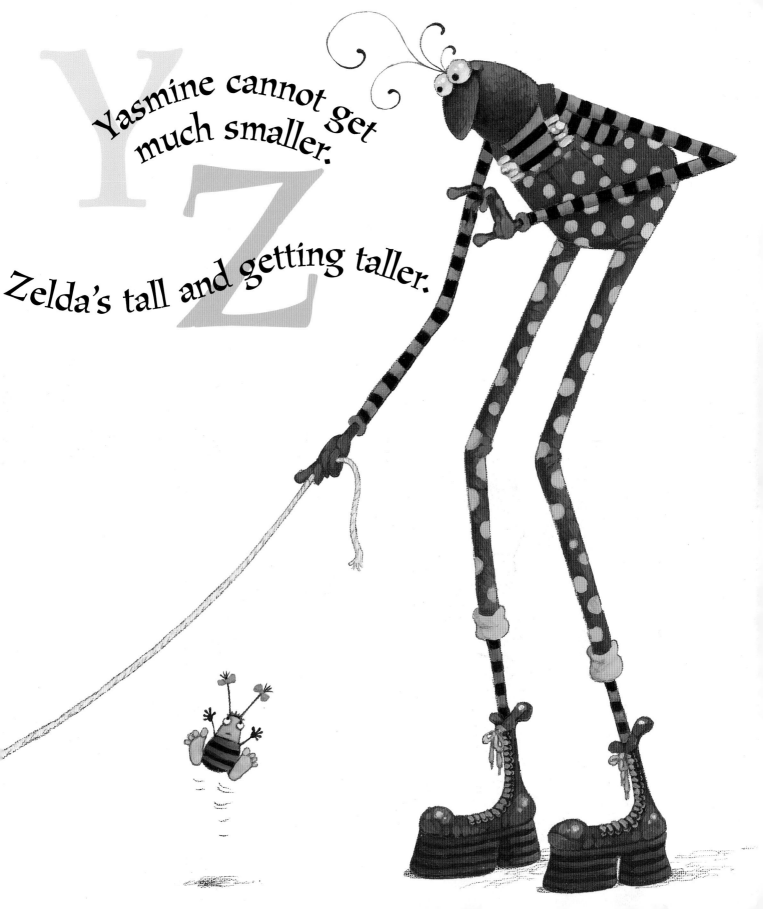

Yasmine cannot get much smaller.

Zelda's tall and getting taller.

These monster children gather 'round
a book their monster teacher found
of creepy creatures A to Z,
to help them learn their ABCs.

And right before the book is done
they spot a REALLY freaky one—

with blinking eyes, a bumpless chin,
roundish ears and furless skin,
a tiny tongue, a weird hairdo
and such a silly body, too!

They scramble for
a better view.